This book is dedicated to my hero.

Though his smile has gone forever
And his hand I cannot touch
This man who was my hero
Is loved so very much

To my Dad, who always told me never give in and you will succeed.

Other titles by the same author:

Betty in the Tower (Zodiac Publishing 2004)

Published by Zodiac Publishing UK

bookorders@zodiacpublishing.org
www.zodiacpublishing.org

First published November 2005

ISBN 1-904566-73-1

Printed by International Printing Press, Dubai

Betty Saves Christmas

By Jan Webber

Illustrations by Amber Dawn Chadwick

At the end of Spandangley Hill, hidden deep inside Frosty Bottom Woods lives Veronica the Fairy and her very best friend, Betty.

Veronica is very good at magic spells, unfortunately, Betty isn't.

It was nearly Christmas and all the fairies, elves and hobgoblins from Frosty Bottom Woods were enjoying themselves at the Fairy Queen's Festive Ball.

Now as I'm sure you know, hobgoblins love a good party and they also love to play tricks on people, especially fairies.

'The party's what?' asked Betty when the two naughty hobgoblins, Mangle and Wurzel, had told her a big fib about the party being cancelled.

'Yes, party's off, party's off,' chanted Mangle and Wurzel as they hopped about pretending to count berries on the holly bush outside Betty's front door.

At that very same time, in a little snow-covered house in the North Pole, Mrs. Claus was having a spot of bother with her washing machine.

Santa's best Christmas outfit had become so small that he would never fit into it.

'Oh no!' said Mrs. Claus, holding up the tiny red coat. 'Maybe I should put Santa on the North Pole diet!'

Mrs. Claus knew she had to call for some help before Santa finished getting ready and asked for his special red suit.

'This is a job for Veronica the Fairy,' Mrs. Claus told Camilla the Reindeer, as she quickly dialled the Fairy Help Line.

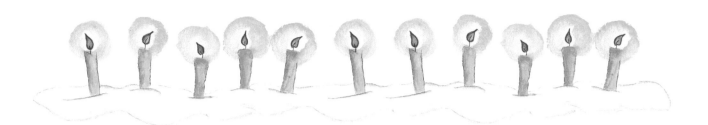

Back at the party, Mariah Fairy was singing her number one hit 'All We Want for Christmas' while everyone waited for the Fairy Queen to give them their very own special Christmas jobs.

Flutter and Flit the Butterfly Fairies had to sprinkle magic sleepy dust over all the children, so that they stayed fast asleep until morning.

Frosty the Snowman had his usual job to do.

But this year he certainly wouldn't let a pesky fairy called Betty throw snowballs at him.

The nine naughty gnomes were given a very special job each, even though they were always up to mischief.

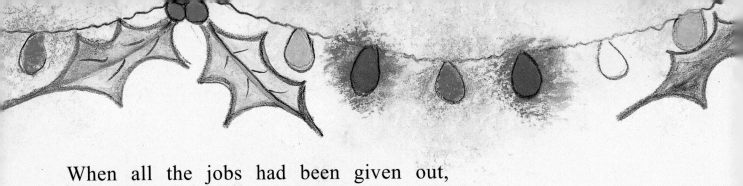

When all the jobs had been given out, Flirtywing the Fairy Queen told Veronica about Mrs. Claus's little problem.

'Oh dear,' said Veronica trying not to laugh. 'I would love to help Mrs. Claus, but my wand has just gone in for a service.'

'I'm sure Betty could manage to get this small job right, just give her a chance.'

Flirtywing doubted that very much, but agreed to let her try.

The Fairy Queen handed Veronica a very special sparkly wand and a giant bag of fairy dust (just in case).

'Just remember to swap Betty's wand for this special one,' Flirtywing said with a wink.

When Veronica arrived home Betty was fast asleep. The naughty hobgoblins had told Betty that the party was cancelled, so she had decided to wash her hair and have an early night.

Veronica very carefully swapped Betty's wand for the special sparkly one.

The next day was Christmas Eve and there was no time to waste.

'Time to get up, time to get up, jobs to do...yes...important jobs to do,' called Stipple and Dab as they threw rosy red holly berries at Betty's window.

Veronica told Betty about the special job she had to do for Mrs. Claus. Betty was so excited that she didn't see the special magic wand that Veronica had secretly slipped under her pillow.

So she tucked her old wand safely into her best Christmas knickers, dusted off her wings and smiled.

'Come on Veronica, let's go!'

Up, up and away they flew, across the starry sky all the way to the North Pole, where Mrs. Claus was getting herself spruced up a little.

Mrs. Claus hoped that when Santa got a whiff of her new "Essence of Mince Pie" perfume, he wouldn't notice that his coat was too tight.

However, things were a little tighter than she thought.

'Mrs. Claus!' boomed Santa.

'IT WAS DRY CLEAN ONLY!'

'Don't worry, dear,' said Mrs. Claus, 'everything's under control. Veronica will be here as quick as a kiss under the mistletoe.'

Mrs. Claus was quite surprised to see Betty arrive with Veronica.

'Ooh look Santa, it's Betty!'

But Betty didn't waste a second. 'Shivering snowmen!' she shouted pulling out the wand that was tucked inside her Christmas undies.

*"Spangley Dangley fiddly toot,
This spell will fix Santa's suit!"*

'Oops! That's not right, I'll try again,' she said.

"This magic suit so red and small,
Just won't fit Santa Claus at all,

Even if he breathes in tight,
He'll never get it on tonight!

So with this magic, (just a bit)
We'll make his suit a perfect fit."

Santa, Mrs. Claus and Veronica all held their
breath. But still nothing happened...

'Oopsie,' said Betty.

Veronica decided it was time to get out the very big box of magic fairy dust that Flirtywing the Fairy Queen had given her in case of an emergency.

Betty decided it might be a good idea to check her magic Fairy Spell Book. 'Oh, here's one that might work.' She giggled and waving her wand, she tried just one more time.

"As snowflakes fall upon the ground,
I cast this magic all around.
Fairy wings and a silver flute,
Will work its magic on Santa's suit.
Tinkling bells on a frosty night,
Is all it takes to make it right!"

'Yipee!' everyone cried as Santa's suit began to get bigger and bigger until it fit him perfectly.

'Ho, ho, ho,' said Santa in his very Father Christmassy voice. 'Looks like tonight will be a magical night after all.'

To Betty,
Merry Christmas!
Love Santa

Inside Santa's grotto, underneath the twinkling Christmas tree was a very special present.

Because after all, Betty did save Christmas!

The End